The True-Born Englishman: A SATYR

Daniel Defoe

Table of Contents

THE True–Born Englishman: A SATYR

Daniel Defoe

Stataimus Pacem, & Securitatem, & Concordiam Judicium & Justitiam inter Anglos & Normannos, Francos, & Britones Walliæ & Cornubiæ, Pictos & Scotos Albaniæ, *similiter inter Francos & Insulanos, Provincias, & Patrias, que pertinent ad Coronam nostram, & inter omnes nobis Subjectos, firmiter & inviolabiliter observari.*

Charta Regis Willielmi Conquisitoris de Pacis Publica, *Cap*. I.

An Explanatory PREFACE.

It is not that I see any Reason to alter my Opinion in any thing I have writ, which occasions this Epistle; but I find it necessary for the satisfaction of some Persons of Honour, as well as Wit, to pass a short Explication upon it, and tell the World what I means, or rather, what I do not mean, in some things wherein I find I am liable to be misunderstood.

I confess my self something surpriz'd to bear that I, am tax'd with Bewraying my own Nest, and Abusing our Nation, by Discovering the Meanness of our Original, in order to make the English *contemptible abroad and at home; in which, I think, they are mistaken:*

1

THE True–Born Englishman: A SATYR

For why should not our Neighbours be as good as We to Derive from? And I must add, That had we been an unmix'd Nation, I am of Opinion it had been to our Disadvantage: For to go no farther, we have three Nations about us as clear from mixtures of Blood as any in the World, and I know not which of them I could with our selves to be like; I mean the Scots, *the* Welsh *and the* Irish; *and if I were to write a Reverse to the* Satyr, *I would examine all the Nations of* Europe, *and prove, That those Nations which are most mix'd, are the best, and have least of Barbarism and Brutality among them; and abundance of Reasons might be given for it, too long to bring into a* Preface.

But I give this Hint, to let the World know, that I am far from thinking, 'tis a Satyr *upon the* English *Nation, to tell them, they are Derived from all the Nations under Heaven; that is,* from several Nations. *Nor is it meant to undervalue the Original of the* English, *for we see no reason to like them worse, being the Relicts of* Romans, Danes, Saxons *and* Normans, *than we should have done if they had remain'd* Britains, *that is,* than if they had been all *Welshmen.*

But the Intent of the Satyr *is pointed at the Vanity of those who talk of their Antiquity, and value themselves upon their Pedigree, their Ancient Families, and being* True–Born; *whereas 'tis impossible we shou'd be* True–Born; *and if we could, shou'd have lost by the Bargain.*

These sort of People, who call themselves True–Born, *and tell long Stories of their Families, and like a Nobleman of* Venice, Think a Foreigner ought not to walk on the same side of the Street with them, *are own'd to be meant in this* Satyr. *What they would infer from their long Original, I know not, nor is it easie to make out whether they are the better or the worse for their Ancestors: Our* English *Nation may Value themselves for their* Wit, Wealth *and* Courage, *and I believe few Nations will dispute it with them; but for long Originals, and Ancient* True–Born *Families of* English, *I wou'd advise them to wave the Discourse. A True English* Man *is one that deserves a Character, and I have no where lessened him, that I know of; but as for a* True Born *English Man,* I confess I do not understand him.

From hence I only infer, That an English *Man, of all Men ought not to despise Foreigners as such, and I think the Inference is just, since* what they are to Day, we were yesterday, and to morrow they will be like us. *If Foreigners misbehave in their several Stations and Employments,* I have nothing to do with that; *the Laws are open to punish them equally with Natives, and let them have no Favour.*

But when I see the Town full of Lampoons and Invectives against Dutchmen, *Only because they are Foreigners, and the King Reproached and Insulted by Insolent Pedants, and Ballad–making Poets, for employing Foreigners, and for being a Foreigner himself, I confess my self moved by it to remind our Nation of their own Original, thereby to let them see what a Banter is put upon our selves in it; since speaking of* Englishmen ab Origine, *we are really all Foreigners our selves.*

I could go on to prove 'Tis also Impolitick in us to discourage Foreigners; since 'tis easie to make it appear that the multitudes of Foreign Nations who have took Sanctuary here, have been the greatest Additions to the Wealth and Strength of the Nation; the greatest Essential whereof is the Number of its Inhabitants: Nor would this Nation have ever arriv'd to the Degree of Wealth and Glory, it now boasts of, if the addition of Foreign Nations, both as to Manufactures and Arms, had not been helpful to it. This is so plain, that he who is ignorant of it is too dull to be talk'd with.

The Satyr therefore I must allow to be just, till I am otherwise convinc'd; because nothing can be more ridiculous than to hear our People boast of that Antiquity, which if it had been true, would have left us in so much worse a Condition than we are in now: Whereas we ought rather to boast among our Neighbours, that we are a part of themselves, of the same Original as they, but better'd by our Climate, and like our Language and Manufactures, deriv'd from them, and improv'd by us to a Perfection greater than they can pretend to.

This we might have valu'd our selves upon without Vanity: But to disown our Descent from them, talk big of our Ancient Families, and long Originals, and stand at a distance from Foreigners, like the Enthusiast in Religion, *with a* Stand off, I am more Holy than thou: *This is a thing so ridiculous, in a Nation deriv'd from Foreigners, as we are, that I could not but attack them as I have done.*

And whereas I am threatned to be call'd to a Publick Account for this Freedom; and the Publisher of this has been News–paper'd *into Goal already for it; tho' I see nothing in it for which the Government can be displeased; yet if at the same time those People who with an unlimited Arrogance in Print, every Day Affront the King, Prescribe the Parliament, and Lampoon the Government, may be either Punished or Restrained, I am*

3

content to stand and fall by the publick Justice of my Native Country, which I am not sensible I have any where injur'd.

Nor would I be misunderstood concerning the Clergy; with whom if I have taken any License more than becomes a Satyr, *I question not but those Gentlemen, who are Men of Letters, are also Men of so much Candor, as to allow me a Loose at the Crimes of the Guilty, without thinking the whole Profession lash'd who are Innocent. I profess to have very mean Thoughts of those Gentlemen who have deserted their own Principles, and expos'd even their Morals as well as Loyalty; but not at all to think it affects any but such as are concern'd in the Fact.*

Nor would I be misrepresented as to the Ingratitude of the English *to the King and his Friends; as if I meant the* English *as a Nation, are so. The contrary is so apparent, that I would hope it should not be Suggested of me: And therefore when I have brought in* Britannia *Speaking of the King, I suppose her to be the Representative or Mouth of the Nation, as a Body. But if I say we are full of such who daily affront the King, and abuse his Friends; who Print scurrilous Pamphlets, virulent Lampoons, and reproachful publick Banters, against both the King's Person and his Government; I say nothing but what is too true: And that the* Satyr *is directed at such, I freely own; and cannot say, but I shou'd think it very hard to be Censur'd for this* Satyr, *while such remain Unqusestion'd and tacitly approv'd. That I can mean none but such, is plain from these few Lines,*

> Ye Heavens regard! Almighty. *Jove,* look down,
> And view thy injur'd Monarch on the Throne.
> On their ungrateful Heads due Vengeance take,
> Who sought his Aid, and then his Part forsake.

If I have fallen rudely upon our Vices, I hope none but the Vicious will be angry. As for Writing for Interest I disown it; I have neither Place *nor* Pension, *nor* Prospect; *nor* seek none, *nor will* have none: *If matter of Fact justifies the Truth of the Crimes, the* Satyr *is just. As to the Poetick Liberties I hope the Crime is pardonable: I am content to be Ston'd, provided none will Attack me but the Innocent.*

If my Country–Men would take the Hint, and grow better Natur'd from my ill–Natur'd *Poem, as some call it; I would say this of it, that thot it is far from the best* Satyr *that ever was Wrote, 'twould do the most Good that ever* Satyr *did.*

And yet I am ready to ask Pardon of some Gentlemen too; who tho' they are English-men, *have good Nature to see themselves Reprov'd, and can bear it. These are Gentlemen in a true Sense, that can bear to be told of their* Faux Pas, *and not abuse the Reprover. To such I must say, this is no* Satyr; *they are Exceptions to the General Rule; and I value my Performance from their Generous Approbation, more than I can from any Opinon I have of its Worth.*

The hasty Errors of my Verse I made my Excuse for before; and since the time I have been upon it has been but little, and my Leisure less, I have all along strove rather to make the Thoughts Explicite, than the Poem Correct. However, I have mended some Faults in this Edition, and the rest must be plac'd to my Account.

As to Answers, Banters, True-English Billinsgate, *I expect them till no body will buy, and then the Shop will be shut. Had I wrote it for the Gain of the Press, I should have been concern'd at its being Printed again and again, by* Pyrates, *as they call them, and* Paragraph- Men: *But would they but do it Justice, and print it True, according to the Copy, they are welcome to sell it for a Penny, if they please.*

The Pence indeed is the End of their Works. I'll engage, if no body will Buy, no body will Write: And not a Patriot Poet of them all now will in Defence of his Native Country, which I have abus'd, they say, *Print an* Answer *to it, and give it about for* God's-sake.

THE PREFACE

The End of Satyr is Reformation: And the Author, tho' he doubts the Work of Conversion is at a General Stop, has put his Hand to the Plow.

I expect a Storm of Ill-language from the Fury of the Town, and especially from those whose English *Talent it is to Rail: And without being taken for a Conjurer, I may venture to foretel, that I shall be Cavil'd at about my* mean Stile, rough Verse, *and incorrect* Language; *Things I might indeed have taken more Care in. But the Book is Printed; and tho I see some Faults, 'tis too late to mend them: And this is all I think needful to say to them.*

Possibly somebody may take me for a Dutchman, *in which they are mistaken: But I am one that would be glad to see* Englishmen *behave themselves better to Strangers, and to Governours also; that one might not be reproached in Foreign Countries for belonging to* a Nation that wants Manners.

I assure you, Gentlemen, Strangers use us better abroad; and we can give no reason but our Ill Nature for the contrary here.

Methinks an Englishman, *who is so proud of being call'd* A Goodfellow, *shou'd be Civil: And it cannot be denied but we are in many Cases, and particularly to Strangers, the churlishest People alive.*

As to Vices, who can dispute our Intemperance, *while an* Honest *Drunken Fellow is a Character in a Mans Praise? All our Reformations are Banters, and will be so, till our Magistrates and Gentry Reform themselves by way of Example; then, and not till then, they may be expected to punish others without Blushing.*

As to our Ingratitude, *I desire to be understood of that particular People, who pretending to be Protestants, have all along endeavour'd to reduce the Liberties and Religion of this Nation into the Hands of King* James *and his Popish Powers: Together, with such who enjoy the Peace and Protection of the present Government, and yet abuse and affront the King who procur'd it, and openly profess their uneasiness under him: These, by whatsoever Names or Titles they are dignified, or distinguish'd, are the People aim'd at: Nor do I disown, but that it is so much the Temper of an* Englishman *to abuse his Benefactor, that I could be glad to see it rectified.*

They who think I have been guilty of any Error, in exposing the Crimes of my own Country–men to themselves, may among many honest Instances of the like nature, find the same thing in Mr Cowly, *in his imitation of the second Olympick Ode of* Pindar: *His Words are these;*

> But in this Thankless World, the Givers
> Are Envy'd even by th'Receivers:

THE True-Born Englishman: A SATYR

'Tis now the Cheap and Frugal Fashion,
Rather to hide than pay an Obligation.
    Nay, 'tis much worse than so;
    It now an *Artifice* doth grow,
    Wrongs and *Outrages* to do,
Left Men should think we *Owe*.

THE INTRODUCTION

Speak, *Satyr*, for there's none can tell like thee,
Whether 'Tis Folly, Pride, or Knavery,
That makes this discontented Land appear
Less happy now in Times of Peace, than War:
Why Civil Feuds disturb the Nation more,
Than all our bloody Wars have done before.
    Fools out of Favour grudge at Knaves in Place,
And Men are always honest in Disgrace:
The Court Preferments make Men Knaves in course:
But they which wou'd be in them, wou'd be worse.
'Tis not at Foreigners that we repine,
Wou'd Foreigners their Perquisites resign:
The Grand Contention's plainly to be seen,
To get some Men put out, and some put in.
For this our Senators make long Harangues.
And florid Members whet their polish'd Tongues,
Statesmen are always sick of one Disease;
And a good Pension gives them present Ease.
That's the Specifick makes them all Content
With any King and any Government.
Good Patriots at Court–Abuses rail,
And all the Nation's Grievances bewail:
But when the *Sov'reign Balsam's* once apply'd,
The Zealot never fails to change his Side.
And when he must the *Golden Key* resign,
The *Railing Spirit* comes about again,

THE True-Born Englishman: A SATYR

Who shall this Bubbl'd Nation disabuse,
While they their own Felicities refuse?
Who at the Wars have made such mighty Pother,
And now are falling out with one another:
With needless Fears the Jealous Nation fill,
And always have been sav'd against their Will:
Who Fifty Millions *Sterling* have disburs'd,
To be with Peace and too much Plenty Curs'd.
Who their Old Monarch eagerly undo,
And yet uneasily obey the New.
Search, *Satyr*, search; a deep Incision make;
The Poyson's strong, the Antidote's too weak.
'Tis pointed Truth must manage this Dispute,
And down−right English *Englishmen* Confute.　Whet thy just Anger at the
Nation's Pride;
And with keen Phrase repel the Vicious Tide.
To *Englishmen* their own beginnings show,
And ask them why they slight their Neighbours so.
Go back to elder Times, and Ages past,
And Nations into long Oblivion cast;
To old *Britannia*'s Youthful Days retire,
And there for *True−Born Englishmen* enquire,
Britannia freely will disown the Name,
And hardly knows her self from whence they came:
Wonders that They of all Men shou'd pretend
To *Birth* and *Blood*, and for a Name contend.
Go back to Causes where our Follies dwell,
And fetch the dark Original from Hell:
Speak, *Satyr*, for there's none like thee can tell.

PART I.

Where−ever God erects a House of Prayer,
The Devil always builds a Chapel there:
And 'twill be found upon Examination,

The latter has the largest Congregation:
For ever since he first debauch'd the Mind,
He made a perfect Conquest of Mankind.
With Uniformity of Service, he
Reigns with a general Aristocracy.
No Nonconforming Sects disturb his Reign,
For of his Yoak there's very few Complain.
He knows the Genius and the Inclination,
And matches proper Sins for every ev'ry Nation.
He needs no Standing–Army Government;
He always Rules us by our own Consent:
His Laws are easie, and his gentle Sway
Makes it exceeding pleasant to obey.
The List of his Vice–gerents and Commanders,
Out–does your *Cæsars*, or your *Alexanders*.
They never fail of his infernal Aid,
And he's as certain ne'er to be betray'd.
Thro' all the World they spread his vast Command,
And death's Eternal Empire is maintain'd.
They rule so politickly and so well,
As if they were Lords Justices of Hell.
Duly divided to debauch Mankind,
And plant Infernal Dictates in his Mind.
    Pride, the first Peer, and President of Hell,
To his share *Spain*, the largest Province, fell.
The subtile Prince thought fittest to bestow
On these the Golden Mines of *Mexico*;
With all the Silver Mountains of *Peru*;
Wealth which would in wise hands the World undo:
Because he knew their Genius to be such;
Too Lazy and too Haughty to be Rich.
So proud a People, so above their Fate,
That if reduc'd to beg, they'll beg in State.
Lavish of Money, to be counted Brave,
And proudly starve, because they scorn to save.
Never was Nation in the World before,

9

THE True-Born Englishman: A SATYR

So very Rich, and yet so very Poor.
   Lust chose the Torrid Zone of *Italy*,
Where Blood ferments in Rapes and Sodomy:
Where swelling Veins o'erflow with livid Streams,
With Heat impregnate from *Vesuvian* Flames:
Whose flowing Sulphur forms Infernal Lakes,
And humane Body of the Soil partakes.
There Nature ever burns with hot Desires,
Fann'd with Luxuriant Air from Subterranean Fires:
Here undisturb'd in Floods of scalding Lust,
Th'Infernal King reigns with Infernal Gust.
   Drunk'nness, the Darling Favourite of Hell,
Chose *Germany* to Rule; and Rules so well,
No Subjects more obsequiously obey,
None please so well, or are so pleas'd as they.
The cunning Artist manages so well,
He lets them Bow to Heav'n, and Drink to Hell.
If but to Wine and him they Homage pay,
He cares not to what Deity they Pray,
What God they worship most, or in what way.
Whether by *Luther, Calvin,* or by *Rome*,
They fail for Heav'n, by Wine he steers them home.   Ungovern'd Passion
settied first in *France*,
   Where Mankind Lives in Haste, and Thrives by Chance,
A *Dancing Nation*, Fickle and Untrue:
Have oft undone themselves, and others too:
Prompt the Infernal Dictates to Obey,
And in Hell's Favour none more great than they.
   The *Pagan* World he blindly leads away,
And Personally Rules with Arbitrary Sway:
The Mask thrown off, *Plain Devil* his Title stands;
And what elsewhere he Tempts, he there Commands,
There with full Gust th'Ambition of his Mind
Governs, as he of old in Heav'n design'd.
Worship'd as God, his *Painim Altars* smoke,
Embru'd with Blood of those that him Invoke,   The rest by Deputies he

10

Rules as well,
    And plants the distant Colonies of Hell.
    By them his Secret Power he well maintains,
    And binds the World in his Infernal Chains.   By Zeal the *Irish*, and the *Rush*
by Folly:
    Fury the *Dame:* The *Swede* by Melancholy:
    By stupid Ignorance the *Muscovite*:
    The Chinese by a *Child of Hell*, call'd Wit;
    Wealth makes the Persian too Effeminate:
    And Poverty the *Tartars* Desperate:
    The *Turks* and *Moors* by *Mah'met* he subdues:
    And God has given him leave to rule the Jews:
    Rage rules the *Portuguese*, and Fraud the *Scotch* :
    Revenge the *Pole*; and Avarice the *Dutch.*   *Satyr* be kind, and draw a silent
Veil,
    Thy *Native England*'s Vices to conceal:
    Or if that Task's impossible to do,
    At least be just, and show her Vertues too;
    Too Great the first, Alas! the last too Few.   *England* unknown as yet,
unpeopled lay;
    Happy, had she remain'd so to this Day,
    And not to ev'ry Nation been a Prey.
    Her open Harbours, and her Fertile Plains,
    The Merchants Glory these, and those the Swains,
  To ev'ry Barbarous Nation have betray'd her,
  Who Conquer her as oft as they Invade her.
  So Beauty Guarded but by Innocence,
  That Ruins her which should be her Defence.
    Ingratitude, a Devil of *Black Renown*,
  Possess'd her very early for his own.
  An Ugly, Surly, Sullen, Selfish Spirit,
  Who Satan's *worst Perfections does Inherit*:
  Second to him in Malice and in Force,
  All *Devil without*, and all *within* him *Worse* .
    He made her First–born Race to be so rude,
  And suffer'd her to be so oft subdu'd:

THE True–Born Englishman: A SATYR

By sev'ral Crowds of wand'ring Thieves o'er–run,
Often unpeopl'd, and as oft undone.
While ev'ry Nation that her Powers reduc'd,
Their Languages and Manners introduc'd.
From whose mix'd Relicks our Compounded Breed,
By Spurious Generation does succeed;
Making a Race uncertain and unev'n,
Deriv'd from all the Nations under Heav'n.
   The *Romans* first with *Julius Cæsar* came,
Including all the Nations of that Name,
Gauls, Greeks, and *Lombards*; and by Computation,
Auxiliaries, or Slaves of ev'ry Nation.
With *Hengist, Saxons*; *Danes* with *Sueno* came,
In search of Plunder, not in search of Fame.
Scots, Picts, and *Irish* from th' *Hibernian* Shore;
And Conqu'ring *William* brought the *Normans o'er* .
   All these their Barb'rous Off–spring left behind,
The Dregs of Armies, they of all Mankind;
Blended with *Britains* who before were here,
Of whom the *Welsh* ha' blest the Character.
   From this Amphibious Ill–born Mob began
That vain ill–natur'd thing, an English–man,
The Customs, Sir–names, Languages, and Manners,
Of all these Nations are their own Explainers:
Whose Relicks are so lasting and so strong,
They ha' left a *Shiboleth* upon our Tongue;
By which with easie search you may distinguish
Your *Roman–Saxon–Danish–Norman* English.
   The great Invading *Norman* let us know
What Conquerors in After–Times might do
To ev'ry *Musqueteer* he brought to *Town*,
He gave the Lands which never were his own.
When first the *English* Crown he did obtain,
He did not send his *Dutchmen* home again.
No Re–assumptions in his Reign were known,
Davenant might there ha' let his Book alone.

THE True–Born Englishman: A SATYR

No Parliament his Army cou'd disband;
He rais'd no Money, for he paid in Land.
He gave his Legions their Eternal Station,
And made them all Free–holders of the Nation.
He Canton'd out the Country to his Men,
And ev'ry Soldier was a Denizen.
The Rascals thus Enrich'd, he call'd them *Lords*,
To please their Upstart Pride with new made Words;
And *Doomsday–Book* his Tyranny Records.
  And here begins our Ancient Pedigree
That so exalts our poor Nobility:
'Tis that from some *French* Trooper they derive,
Who with the *Norman* Bastard did arrive:
The Trophies of the Families appear;
Some show the Sword, the Bow, and some the Spear,
Which their Great Ancestor, *forsooth*, did wear.
These in the Herald's Register remain,
Their Noble mean Extraction to explain.
Yet who the Heroe was, no Man can tell,
Whether a Drummer or a Colonel:
The silent Record Blushes to reveal
Their Undescended Dark Original.
  But grant the best, How came the Change to pass;
A True–Born Englishman of Norman Race?
A Turkish Horse can show more History,
To prove his Well–descended Family.
Conquest, as by the Moderns 'Tis exprest,
May give a Title to the Lands possest:
But that the Longest Sword shou'd be so Civil,
To make a *Frenchman English*, that's the Devil.   These are the Heroes who
despise the *Dutck*,
  And rail at new–come Foreigners so much;
Forgetting that themselves are all deriv'd
From the most Scoundrel Race that ever liv'd,
A horrid Crowd of Rambling Thieves and Drones;
Who ransack'd Kingdoms, and dispeopled Towns.

THE True-Born Englishman: A SATYR

The *Pict* and Painted *Britain*, Treach'rous *Scot*,
By Hunger, Theft, and Rapine, hither brought.
Norweigian Pirates, Buccaneering *Danes*,
Whose Red-hair'd Off-spring ev'ry where remains.
Who join'd with *Norman-French* compound the Breed
From whence your *True Born Englishmen* proceed.   And left by Length of
Time it be pretended,
The Climate may this Modern Breed ha' mended;
Wife Providence to keep us where we are,
Mixes us daliy with exceeding Care:
We have been *Europe*'s Sink, the *Jakes* where she
Voids all her Offal Out-cast Progeny.
From our Fifth *Henry's* time, the Strolling Bands
Of banish'd Fugitives from Neighb'ring Lands,
Have here a certain Sanctuary found:
Th' Eternal Refuge of the Vagabond.
Where in but half a common Age of Time,
Borr'wing new Blood and Manners from the Clime,
Proudly they learn all Mankind to contemn,
And all their Race are *True-Born Englishmen.*
  Dutch, Walloons, Flemmings, Irishmen, and *Scots*,
Vaudois and *Valtolins*, and *Hugonots*,
In good Queen *Bess's* Charitable Reign,
Supply'd us with three hundred thousand Men.
Religion, *God we thank thee*, sent them hither,
Priests, Protestants, the Devil and all together:
Of all Professions, and of ev'ry Trade,
All that were persecuted or afraid;
Whether for Debt, or other Crimes they fled,
David at *Hackelah* was still their Head.   The Off-spring of this Miscellaneous
Crowd,
Had not their new Plantations long enjoy'd,
But they grew *Englishmen*, and rais'd their Votes
At Foreign Shoals of *Interloping Scots*.
The Royal Branch from *Pict-land* did succeed,
With Troops of *Scots*, and Scabs from *North-by-Tweed*.

14

THE True–Born Englishman: A SATYR

The Seven first Years of his Pacifick Reign
Made him and half his Nation *Englishmen*.
Scots from the *Northern* Frozen Banks of *Tay*,
With Packs and Plods came *Whigging* all away:
Thick as the Locusts which in *Ægypt* swarn'd,
With Pride and hungry Hopes compleatly arm'd:
With Native *Truth, Diseases*, and no *Money*,
Plunder'd our *Canaan* of the Milk and Honey.
Here they grew quickly Lords and Gentlemen,
And all their Race are *True–Born*–Englishmen.
    The Civil Wars, the common Purgative,
Which always use to make the Nation thrive,
Made way for all that strolling Congregation,
Which throng'd in Pious *Ch—s*'s Restoration.
The *Royal Refugee* our Breed restores,
With *Foreign Courtiers*, and with *Foreign Whores* :
And carefully repeopled us again,
Throughout his Lazy, Long, Lascivious Reign;
With such a blest and True–born *English* Fry,
As much Illustrates our Nobility.
A Gratitude which will so black appear,
As future Ages must abhor to hear:
When they look back on all that Crimson Flood,
Which stream'd in *Lindsey's*, and *Caernarvon*'s Blood:
Bold *Strafford, Cambridge, Capel, Lucas, Lisle*,
Who crown'd in Death his Father's Fun'ral Pile.
The loss of whom, in order to supply,
With *True–Born*–English Nobility,
Six Bastard Dukes survive his Luscious Reign,
The Labours of *Italian Castlemain*,
French Portsmouth, Taby Scot, and Cambrian.
Besides the Num'rous Bright and Virgin Throng,
Whole Female Glories shade them from my Song.
sp;   This Off–spring, if one Age they multiply,
May half the House with *English* Peers supply:
There with true *English* Pride they may contemn

15

THE True-Born Englishman: A SATYR

Schomberg and *Portland*, new made Noblemen.   *French* Cooks, *Scotch*
Pedlars, and *Italian* Whores,
    Were all made Lords, or Lords Progenitors.
    Beggars and Bastards by his new Creation,
    Much multiply'd the P—ge of the Nation;
    Who will be all, e'er one short Age runs o'er,
    As *True—Born* Lords as those we had before—   Then to recruit the Commons
he prepares,
    And heal the Latent Breaches of the Wars;
    The Pious Purpose better to advance,
    H'invites the banish'd Protestants of *France*:
    Hither for Gods—sake and their own they fled,
    Some for Religion came, and some for Bread:
    Two hundred Thousand Pair of Wooden Shooes,
    Who, God be thank'd had nothing left to lose;
    To Heav'n's great Praise did for Religion fly,
    To make us starve our Poor in Charity.
    In ev'ry Port they plant their fruitful Train,
    To get a Race of *True—Born* Englishmen:
    Whose Children will, when Riper Years they see,
    Be as Ill—natur'd and as Proud as we:
    Call themselves *English*, Foreigners despise,
    Be Surly like us all, and just as Wise.
      Thus from a Mixture of all Kinds began,
    That Het'rogeneous *Thing, An Englishman*:
    In eager Rapes, and furious Lust begot,
    Betwixt a Painted *Britain* and a *Scot*.
    Whose gend'ring Off—spring quickly learn'd to Bow,
    And yoke their Heifers to the *Roman* Plough:
    From whence a Mongrel half—Bred Race there came,
    With neither Name, nor Nation, Speech or Fame.
    In whose hot Veins new Mixtures quickly ran,
    Insus'd betwixt a *Saxon* and a *Dane*.
    While their Rank Daughters, to their Parents just,
    Receiv'd all Nations with Promiscuous Lust.
    This Nauseous Brood directly did contain

THE True–Born Englishman: A SATYR

The well extracted Blood of *Englishmen*.
   Which Medly canton'd in a Heptarchy,
A Rhapsody of Nations to supply,
Among themselves maintain'd eternal Wars,
And still the Ladies Lov'd the Conquerors.
   The *Western* Angles all the rest subdu'd;
A bloody Nation, barbarous and rude:
Who by the *Tenure* of the Sword possest
One part of *Britain*, and subdu'd the rest.
And as great things denominate the small,
The Conqu'ring part gave *Title* to the whole.
The *Scot, Pict, Britain, Roman, Dane*, submit,
And with the *English–Saxon* all Unite:
And these the mixture have so close pursu'd,
The very Name and Memory's subdu'd:
No *Roman* now, no *Britain* does remain;
Wales strove to separate, but strove in Vain:
The silent Nations undistinguish'd fall,
And *Englishman*'s the common Name for all.
Fate jumbled them together, *God knows how*;
   What e'er they were they're *True–Born English* now. The Wonder which
remains is at our Pride,
   To value that which all wife Men deride.
For *Englishmen* to boast of Generation,
Cancels their Knowledge, and Lampoons the Nation.
A *True–Born Englishman*'s a Contradiction,
In Speech an Irony, in Fact a Fiction.
A Banter made to be a test of Fools,
Which those that use it justly ridicules.
A Metaphor invented to express
A Man *a–kin* to all the Universe.
   For as the *Scots*, as Learned Men ha'said,
Throughout the World their Wand'ring Seed ha'spread;
So open–handed *England*, 'tis Believ'd,
Has all the Gleanings of the World Receiv'd.
   Some think of *England* 'twas our Saviour meant,

17

THE True–Born Englishman: A SATYR

The Gospel should to all the World be sent:
Since, when the Blessed Sound did hither reach,
They to all Nations might be faid to Preach.
   'Tis well that Virtue gives Nobility,
How shall we else the want of Birth and Blood supply?
Since scarce one Family is left alive,
Which does not from some Foreigner derive.
Of sixty thousand *English* Gentlemen,
Whose Names and Arms in Registers remain,
We challenge all our Heralds to declare
Ten Families which *English Saxons* are.

sp;   *France* justly boasts the Ancient Noble Line
Of *Bourbon, Mommorency*, and *Lorrain*.
The *Germans* too their House of *Austria* show,
And *Holland* their Invincible *Nassau*.
Lines which in Heraldry were ancient grown,
Before the Name of *Englishman* was known.
Even *Scotland* too, her Elder Glory shows,
Her *Gourdons, Hamiltons*, and her *Monroes*;
Douglas, Mackays, and *Grahams*, Names well known,
Long before Ancient *England* knew her own.
   But *England*, Modern to the last degree,
Borrows or makes her own Nobility,
And yet the boldly boasts of Pedigree:
Repines that Foreigners are put upon her,
And talks of her Antiquity and Honour:
Her *S—lls, S—ls, C—ls, De—la , M—rs*,
M—ns and *M—ues, D—s*, and *V—rs*,
Not one have *English* Names, yet all are *English* Peers.
Your *Houblons, Papillons*, and *Lethuliers*,
Pass now for *True–born–English* Knights and Squires,
And make good Senate Members, or Lord–Mayors.
Wealth, howsoever got, in *England* makes
Lords of Mechanicks, Gentlemen of Rakes:
Antiquity and Birth are needless here;
'Tis Impudence and Money makes a P—r.

18

THE True–Born Englishman: A SATYR

Innumerable City–Knights we know,
From *Blewcoat–Hospitals* and *Bridewel* flow.
Draymen and Porters fill the City Chair,
And Foot–Boys Magisterial Purple wear.
Fate has but very small Distinction set
Betwixt the *Counter* and the Coronet.
Tarpaulin L—ds, Pages of high Renown,
Rise up by Poor Mens Valour, not their own.
Great Families of yesterday we show,
And Lords, whose Parents were *the Lord knows who*.

PART II.

The Breed's describ'd: Now, *Satyr*, if you can,
Their Temper show, for *Manners make the Man*.
Fierce, as the *Britain*; as the *Roman* Brave;
And less inclin'd to Conquer, than to Save:
Eager to Fight, and lavish of their Blood;
And equally of *Fear and Forecast* void.
The *Pict* has made 'em Sowre, the *Dane* Morose:
False from the *Scot,* and from the *Norman* worse.
What Honesty they have, the *Saxons* gave them.
And That, now they grow old, begins to leave them.
The Climate makes them Terrible and Bold;
And *English* Beef their Courage does uphold:
No Danger can their Daring Spirit pall,
Always provided that their Belly's full.
  In close Intrigues their Faculty's but weak,
For gen'rally whate're they know they speak:
And often their own Councils undermine,
By their Infirmity, and not Design;
From whence the Learned say it does proceed,
That *English* Treasons never can succeed,
For they're so open–hearted, you may know
Their own most secret Thoughts, and others too.

THE True–Born Englishman: A SATYR

The Lab'ring Poor, in spight of Double Pay,
'Are Sawcy, Mutinous, and Beggarly:
So lavish of their Money and their Time,
That want of Forecast is the Nation's Crime.
Good Drunken Company is their Delight;
And what they get by Day they spend by Night.
Dull Thinking seldom does their Heads engage,
But Drink their Youth away, and Hurry on Old Age.
Empty of all good Husbandry and Sense;
And void of Manners most, when void of Pence.
Their strong aversion to Behaviour's such,
They always talk too little, or too much.
So dull, they never take the pains to think:
And seldom are good–natur'd, *but in Drink.*   In *English* Ale their dear
Enjoyment lies,
For which they'll starve themselves and Families
An *Englishman* will fairly Drink as much
As will maintain two Families of *Dutch*:
Subjecting all their Labour to their Pots;
The greatest Artists are the greatest Sots.   The Country poor do by Example
live,
The Gentry lead them, and the Clergy drive;
What may we not from such Examples hope?
The Landlord is their God, the Priest their Pope.
A Drunken Clergy, and a Swearing Bench,
Has giv'n the Reformation such a Drench,
As wise Men think there is some cause to doubt,
Will Purge good Manners and Religion out.   Nor do the Poor alone their
Liquor prize,
The Sages join in this great Sacrifice.
The Learned Men who study *Aristotle*,
Correct him with an Explanation Bottle;
Praise *Epicurus* rather than *Lysander*,
And *Aristippus* more than *Alexander*
The Doctors too their *Galen* here resign,
And gen'rally prescribe *Specifick Wine.*

THE True–Born Englishman: A SATYR

The Graduates Study's grown an easier *Task*,
While for the *Urinal* they toss the *Flask*.
The Surgeon's Art grows plainer ev'ry Hour,
And Wine's the Balm which into Wounds they pour.   *Poets long since*
Parnassus have forsaken,
    And say the ancient Bards were all mistaken.
Apollo's lately abdicate and fled,
    And good King *Bacchus* governs in his stead;
He does the Chaos of the Head refine,
    And Atom–Thoughts jump into Words by Wine:
The Inspiration's of a finer Nature;
    As Wine must needs excel *Parnassus* Water.   *Statesmen their weighty*
Politicks refine,
    And Soldiers raise their Courages by Wine;
Cæcilia gives her Choristers their Choice,
    And let's them all drink Wine to clear their Voice.   *Some think the Clergy*
first found out the way,
    And Wine's the only Spirit by which they Pray.
But others, less prophane than so, agree,
    It clears the Lungs and helps the Memory:
And therefore all of them Divinely think,
    Instead of Study, 'Tis as well to Drink.

    And here I would be very glad to know,
Whether our *Asgilites* may drink or no.
Th'Englightning Fumes of Wine would certainly,
    Assist them much *when they begin to fly*:
Or if a Fiery Chariot shou'd appear,
    Inflam'd by Wine, they'd ha'the less to fear.

    Even the Gods themselves, as Mortals say,
Were they on Earth, wou'd be as drunk as they:
Nectar would be no more Celestial Drink,
    They'd all take *Wine*, to teach them how to think.
But *English* Drunkards, Gods and Men out–do,
    Drink their Estates away, and Senses too.
Colon's in Debt, and if his Friends should fail
    To help him out, must Die at last in Goal;

THE True-Born Englishman: A SATYR

His *Wealthy Uncle* sent a Hundred Nobles,
To pay his trifles off, and rid him of his troubles:
But *Colon* like a *True—Born—Englishman*,
Drank all the Money out in bright Champain;
   And *Colon* does in Custody remain,
Drunk'ness has been the Darling of the Realm,
E'er since a Drunken Pilot bad the Helm.
   In their Religion they are so unev'n,
That each Man goes *his own By—way to Heaven.*
Tenacious of Mistakes to that degree,
That ev'ry Man pursues it sep'rately,
And fancies none can find the Way but he:
So shy of one another they are grown,
As if they strove to get to Heav'n alone.
Rigid and Zealous, Positive and Grave,
And ev'ry Grace, but Charity, they have:
This makes them so Ill—natur'd and Uncivil,
That all Men think an *Englishman* the Devil.
   Surly to Strangers, Froward to their Friend;
Submit to Love with a reluctant Mind,
Resolv'd to be Ungrateful and Unkind.
If by Necessity reduc'd to ask,
The Giver has the difficultest Task:
For what's bestow'd they aukwardly receive,
And always take less freely than they give.
The Obligation is their highest Grief;
And never Love, where they accept Relief.
So sullen in their Sorrows, that 'Tis known,
Tey'll rather die than their Afflictions own:
And if reliev'd, it is too often true,
That they'll abuse their Benefactors too:
For in Distress their Haughty Stomach's such,
They hate to see themselves oblig'd too much,
Seldom Contented, often in the Wrong;
Hard to be Pleas'd at all, and never long.
   If your Mistakes their Ill—Opinion gain,

THE True–Born Englishman: A SATYR

No Merit can their Favour re–obtain:
And if they're not Vindictive in their Fury,
'Tis their Unconstant Temper does secure–ye;
Their Brain's so cool, their Passion seldom burns:
For all's condens'd before the Flame returns:
The Fermentation's of so weak a Matter,
The Humid damps the Fume, and runs it all to Water.
So tho' the Inclination may be strong,
They're Pleas'd by fits, and never Angry long.
   Then if Good Nature shows some slender Proof,
They riever think they have Reward enough;
But like our *Modern Quakers* of the Town,
Expect your Manners, and Return you none.
   Friendship, th' abstracted Union of the Mind,
Which all Men seek, but very few can find:
Of all the Nations in the Universe,
None talk on't more, or understand it less:
For if it does their Property annoy,
Their Property their Friendship will destroy.
   As you discourse them, you shall hear them tell
All things in which they think they do excel:
No Panegyrick needs their Praise record;
An Englishman *ne'er wants his own good word.*
His long Discourses gen'rally appear
Prologu'd with his own wond'rous Character:
But first t'illustrate his own good Name,
He never fails his Neighbour to defame:
And yet he really designs no wrong;
His Malice goes no further than his Tongue.
But Pleas'd to Tattle, he delights to Rail,
To satisfie the Letch'ry of a Tale.
His own dear Praises close the ample Speech,
Tells you how Wise he is; *that is, how Rich*:
For Wealth is Wisdom; he that's Rich is Wise;
And all Men Learned Poverty Despise.
His Generosity comes next, and then

THE True-Born Englishman: A SATYR

Concludes that he's a *True-Born-Englishman*;
And they 'tis known, are Generous and Free,
Forgetting, and Forgiving Injury:
Which may be true, thus rightly understood,
Forgiving Ill turns, and forgetting Good.

  Chearful in Labour when they've undertook it,
But out of Humour, when they're out of Pocket.
But if their Belly, and their Pocket's full,
They may be Phlegmatick, but never Dull:
And if a Bottle does their Brains refine,
It makes their Wit as sparkling as their Wine.   As for the general Vices which
we find
They're guilty of in common with Mankind,
Satyr, forbear, and silently endure;
We must conceal the Crimes we cannot cure.
Nor shall my Verse the brighter Sex defame;
For *English* Beauty will preserve her Name.
Beyond dispute, Agreeable and Fair,
And Modester than other Nations are:
For where the Vice prevails, the great Temptation
Is want of Money more than Inclination.
In general, this only is allow'd,
They're something Noisy, and a little Proud.   An *Englishman* is gentlest in
Command,
Obedience is a Stranger in the Land:
Hardly subjected to the Magistrate;
For Englishmen *do all Subjection hate.*
Humblest when Rich, but peevish when they're Poor:
And think whate'er they have, they merit more.

  The meanest *English* Plow-man studies Law,
And keeps thereby the Magistrates in Awe;
Will boldly tell them what they ought to do,
And sometimes punish their Omissions too.

  Their Liberty and Property's so dear,
They Scorn their Laws or Governours to fear:
So bugbear'd with the Name of Slavery,

24

THE True–Born Englishman: A SATYR

They can't submit to their own Liberty.
Restraint from Ill, is Freedom to the Wise;
But Englishmen *do all Restraint Despise.*
Slaves to the Liquor, Drudges to the Pots,
The Mob are Statesmen, and their Statesmen Sots.   Their Governours they
count such dangerous things,
That 'Tis their Custom to affront their Kings:
So jealous of the Power their Kings possess'd,
They suffer neither Power nor Kings to rest.
The Bad with Force they eagerly subdue;
The Good with constant Clamours they pursue:
And did King Jesus Reign, they'd murmur too.
A discontented Nation, and by far
Harder to Rule in Times of Peace than War:
Easily set together by the Ears,
And full of causeless Jealousies and Fears:
Apt to Revolt, and willing to Rebel,
And never are contented when they're well.
No Government cou'd ever please them long,
Cou'd tie their Hands, or rectifie their Tongue.
In this to Ancient Israel well compar'd,
Eternal Murmurs are among them heard.

It was but lately that they were opprest,
Their Rights invaded, and their Laws supprest:
When nicely tender of their Liberty,
Lord! What a Noise they made of Slavery.
In daily Tumults show'd their Discontent;
Lampoon'd their King, and mock'd his Government:
And if in Arms they did not first appear,
'Twas want of Force, and not for want of Fear.
In humbler Tone than *English* us'd to do,
At Foreign Hands, for Foreign Aid they fue.
William, *the Great Successor of* Nassau,
Their Prayers heard, and their Oppressions saw:
He saw and sav'd them: God and Him they prais'd;
To this their Thanks, to that their Trophies rais'd.

25

But glutted with their own Felicities,
They soon their New Deliverer Despise;
Say all their Prayers back, their Joy disown,
Unsing their Thanks, and pull their Trophies down:
Their Harps of Praise are on the Willows hung;
For Englishmen *are ne'er Contented long.*   The Rev'rend Clergy too! and who'd ha' thought
That they who had such Non–Resistance taught,
Should e'er to Arms against their Prince be brought?
Who up to Heaven did Regal Pow'r advance;
Subjecting *English* Laws to Modes of *France.*
Twisting Religion so with Loyalty,
As one cou'd never Live, and t'other Die.
And yet no sooner did their Prince design
Their Glebes and Perquisites to undermine,
But all their Passive Doctrines laid aside;
The Clergy their own Principles deny'd;
Unpreach'd their Non–resisting Cant, and Pray'd
To Heaven for Help, and to the *Dutch* for Aid.
The Church chim'd all her Doctrines back again,
And Pulpit Champions did the Cause maintain;
Flew in the Face of all their former Zeal,
And Non–Resistance did at once repeal.
   The *Rabbies* say it would be too prolix,
To tie Religion up to Politicks:
The Churches Safety is Suprema Lex.
And so by a new Figure of their own,
Their former Doctrines all at once disown.
As Laws *Post Facto* in the Parliament,
In urgent Cases have obtain'd Assent;
But are as dangerous Presidents laid by;
Made Lawful only by Necessity.
   The Rev'rend Fathers then in Arms appear,
And Men of God became the Men of War.
The Nation, *Fir'd by them*, to Arms apply,
Assault their Antichristian Monarchy;

THE True–Born Englishman: A SATYR

To their due Channel all our Laws restore,
And made things what they shou'd ha' been before.
But when they came to fill the Vacant Throne,
And the *Pale Priests* look'd back on what they'd done;
How *English* Liberty began to thrive,
And Church of *England* Loyalty out–Live:
How all their persecuting Days were done,
And their Deliv'rer plac'd upon the Throne:
The Priests, *as Priests are wont to do*, turn'd Tail:
They're *Englishmen*, and *Nature will prevail*.
Now they deplore the Ruins they ha' made,
And murmur for the Master they betray'd.
Excuse those Crimes they con'd not make him mend;
And suffer for the Cause they can't defend.
Pretend they'd not have carried things so high;
And Proto–Martyrs make for Popery.
Had the Prince done as they design'd the thing,
Ha' set the Clergy up to Rule the King;
Taken a *Donative* for coming hither,
And so ha' left their King and them together,
We had say they, been now a happy Nation.
No doubt we 'd seen a Blessed Reformation:
For Wise Men say 't's as dangerous a thing,
A Ruling Priest–hood, as a Priest–rid King.
And of all Plagues with which Mankind are Curst,
Ecclesiastick Tyranny's the worse.

If all our former Grevances were feign'd,
King *James* has been abus'd, and we trapan'd;
Bugbear'd with Popery and Power Despotick,
Tyrannick Goverment, and Leagues Exotick:
The Revolution's a Phanatick Plot,
W—a Tyrant, and *K*—*J*—was not:
A Factious Army, and a Poyson'd Nation,
Unjustly forc'd King *James's* Abdication.

But if he did the Subjects Rights invade,
Then he was punish'd only, not betray'd,

THE True–Born Englishman: A SATYR

And punishing of King's is no such Crime,
But Englishmen *ba' done it many a Time.*   When Kings the Sword of Justice
first lay down,
They are no Kings, though they possess the Crown.
Titles are Shadows, Crowns are empty things,
The Good of Subjects is the End of Kings;
To guide in War, and to protect in Peace:
Where Tyrants once commence the Kings do cease:
For Arbitrary Power's so strange a thing,
It makes the *Tyrant*, and unmakes the King.
   If Kings by Foreign Priests and Armies Reign,
And Lawless Power against their Oaths maintain,
Then Subjects must ha' reason to complain.
If Oaths must bind us when our Kings do Ill;
To call in Foreign Aid is to Rebel.
By force to circumscribe our Lawful Prince;
Is wilful Treason in the largest Sense:
And they who once Rebel, most certainly
Their God, and Kind, and former Oaths defy.
If we allow no Male–Administration
Could cancel the Allegiance of the Nation:
Let all our Learned Sons of *Levi* try,
This Ecclesastick Riddle to unty:
How they could make a Step to Call the Prince,
And yet pretend to Oaths and Innocence.
   By th' first Address they made beyond the Seas,
They're Perjur'd in the most intense Degrees;
And without Scruple for the time to come,
May Swear to all the Kings in *Christendom*.
And truly did our Kings consider all,
They'd never let the Clergy swear at all:
Their Politick Allegiance they'd refuse;
For Whores and Priests will never want Excuse.   But if the *Mutual Contract*
was dissolv'd,
The Doubts explain'd, the Difficulty solv'd:
That Kings when they descend to Tyranny,

28

THE True–Born Englishman: A SATYR

Dissolve the Bond, and leave the Subject free.
The Government's ungirt, when Justice dies,
And Consitutions are Non–Entities.
The Nation's all a Mob, there's no such thing
As Lords or Commons Parliament or King.
A great promiscuous Croud the Hydra lies,
Till Laws revive, and mutual Contract ties:
A Chaos free to chuse for their own share,
What Case of Government they please to wear.
If to a King they do the Reins commit,
All Men are bound in Conscience to submit:
But then that King must by his Oath assent
To *Postulata's* of the Government;
Which if he breaks, he cuts off the Entail,
And Power retreats to its Original.

   This Doctrine has the Sanction of Assent,
From Nature's Universal Parliment.
The Voice of Nations, and the Course of Things,
Allow that Laws superior are to Kings.
None but Delinquents would have Justice cease,
Knaves rail at Laws, as Soldiers rail at Peace:
For Justice is the End of Government,
As Reason is the Test of Argument.

   No Man was ever yet so void of Sense,
As to Debate the Right of Self–Defence,
A Principle so grafted in the Mind,
With Nature born, and does like Nature bind:
Twisted with Reason and with Nature too;
As neither one nor t'other can undo.

   Nor can this Right be less when National;
Reason which governs one, should govern all.
Whate'er the Dialect of Courts may tell,
He that his Right Demands, can ne'er Rebel.
Which Right, if 'Tis by Governours deny'd,
May be procur'd by Force, or Foreign Aid.
For Tyranny's a Nation's Term of Grief;

THE True–Born Englishman: A SATYR

As Folks cry *Fire*, so hasten in Relief.
And when the hated Word is heard about,
All Men shou'd come to help the People out.
  Thus *England* cry'd *Britannia*'s Voice was heard;
And great *Nassau* to rescue her appear'd:
Call'd by the Universal Voice of Fate;
God and the Peoples Legal Magistrate.
Ye Heav'ns regard! Almighty *Jove*, look down.
And view thy injur'd Monarch on the Throne.
On their Ungrateful Heads due Vengeance take,
Who sought his Aid, and then his aid forsake.
Witness, ye Powers! It was our Call alone,
Which now our Pride makes us asham'd to own.
Britannia's troubles fetch'd him from afar,
To Court the dreadful Casualties of War:
But where Requital never can be made,
Acknowledgment's a Tribute seldom pay'd.
  He dwelt in Bright *Maria's* Circling Arms,
Defended by the Magick of her Charms,
From Foreign Fears, and from Domestick Harms.
Ambition found no Fuel for her Fire,
He had what God cou'd give, or Man desire.
Till *Pity* rowz'd him from his soft Repose:
His Life to unseen Hazards to expose;
Till *Pity* mov'd him in our Cause t' appear;
Pity! *That Word which now we hate to hear.*
But *English* Gratitude is always such,
To hate the Hand which does oblige too much.
  Britannia's Cries gave Birth to his Intent,
And hardly gain'd his unforeseen Assent:
His boding Thoughts foretold him he should find
The People Fickle, Selfish and Unkind.
Which Thought did to his Royal Heart appear
More dreadful than the Dangers of the War:
For nothing grates a generous Mind so soon,
As base Returns for hearty Service done.

THE True–Born Englishman: A SATYR

Satyr be silent, awfully prepare,
Britannia's Song, and *William's* Praise to hear.
Stand by, and let her chearfully rehearse,
Her Grateful Vows in her Immortal Verse.
Loud Fame's Eternal Trumpet let her found:
Listen ye distant Poles, and endless Round.
May the strong Blast the welcome News convey
As far as Sound can reach, or Spirit can fly.
To *Neighb'ring Worlds*, if such there be, relate
Our Hero's Fame, for theirs to imitate.
To distant Worlds of Spirits let her rehearse:
For Spirits without the helps of Voice Converse.
May Angels hear the gladsome News on high,
Mix'd with their everlasting Symphony.
And Hell it self stand in Suspence to know,
Whether it be the Fatal Blast, or no.

BRITANNIA.

The Fame of Vertue 'Tis for which I sound,
And Heroes with Immortal Triumphs Crown'd.
Fame built on solid Vertue swifter flies,
Than Morning–Light can spread my Eastern Skies.
The gatb'ring Air returns the doubling Sound,
And loud repeating Thunders–force it round:
Ecchoes return from Caverns of the Deep:
Old Chaos Dreams on't in Eternal Sleep.
Time hands it forward to its latest Urn,
From whence it never, never shall return;
Nothing is heard so far, or lasts so long;
'Tis beard by ev'ry Ear, and spoke by ev'ry Tongue.   *My Hero, with the Sails of*
Honour Furl'd,
Rises like the Great Genius of the World.
By Fate and Fame wisely prepard to be
The Soul of War, and Life of Victory.
He spreads the Wings of Vertue on the Throne,
And ev'ry Wind of Glory *fans them on.*
Immortal Trophies dwell upon his Brow,

THE True–Born Englishman: A SATYR

Fresh as the Garlands be has won but now.

*   By different Steps the high Assent he gains,*
And differently that high Assent maintains.
Princes for Pride, and Lust, of Rule *make War ;*
And struggle for the Name of Conqueror.
Some Fight for Fame, and some for Victory;
He Fights to Save, and Conquers to set Free.

*   Then seek no Phrase his Titles to conceal,*
And hide with Words what Actions must reveal.
No Parallel from Hebrew *Stories take,*
Of God–like Kings my Similies to make:
No borrow'd Names conceal my living Theam;
But Names and Things directly I proclaim.
His honest Merit does his Glory raise;
Whom that Exalts, let no Man fear to Praise;
Of such a Subject no Man need be shy;
Vertue's above the Reach of Flattery.
He needs no Character, but his own Fame,
Nor any flattering Titles, but his own Name.
William'*s the Name that's spoke by ev'ry Tongue;*
William's the Darling Subject of my Song.
Listen ye Virgins to the Charming Sound,
And in Eternal Dances hand it round:
Your early Offerings to this Altar bring;
Make him at once a Lover and a King.
May be submit to none but to your Arms;
Nor ever be subdu'd, but by your Charms.
May your soft Thoughts for him be all Sublime;
And ev'ry tender Vow be made for him.
May he be first in ev'ry Morning–Thought,
And Heav'n ne'er bear a Pray'r, when he's lest out,
May ev'ry Omen, ev'ry boding Dream,
Be Fortunate *by mentioning his Name;*
May this one Charm Infernal Powers affright,
And guard you from the Terrors of the Night.
May every chearful Glass, as it goes down,

THE True-Born Englishman: A SATYR

To William'*s Health*, be Cordials to your own.
Let ev'ry Song be Chorust with his Name,
And Musick pay her Tribute to his Fame,;
Let ev'ry Poet tune his Artful Verse,
And in Immortal Streins his Deeds rchearse.
And may Apollo *never more inspire*
The Disobedient Bard with his Seraphick Fire.
May all my Sons their grateful Homage pay;
His Praises sing, and for his Safety pray.

   Satyr return to our Unthankful Isle,
Secur'd by Heavens Regard, and *William's* Toil.
To both Ungreateful, and to both Untrue;
Rebels to God, and to Good Nature too.

   If e'er this Nation be Distress'd again,
To whomsoe'er they cry, they'll cry in vain.
To Heav'n they cannot have the Face to look:
Or if they should, it would but Heaven provoke.
To hope for Help from Man would be too much;
Mankind would always tell 'em of the Dutch:
How they came here our Freedoms to maintain,
Were *Paid*, and *Curs'd*, and *Hurry'd home again.*
How by their Aid we first dissolv'd our Fears,
And then our Helpers damn'd for Foreigners.
'Tis not our *English* Temper to do better;
For *Englishmen* think ev'ry Man their Debtor.

   'Tis worth observing, that we ne'er complain'd
Of Foreigners, nor of the Wealth they gain'd,
Till all their Services were at an end
Wise Men affirm it is the *English* way,
Never to Grumble till they come to Pay;
And then they always think, their Temper's such,
The Work too little, and the Pay too much.

   As frighted Patients, when they want a Cure,
Bid any Price, and any Pain endure:
But when the Doctor's Remedies appear,
The Cure's too Easie, and the Price too Dear.

THE True–Born Englishman: A SATYR

    Great. *Portland* ne'er was banter'd when he strove
For Us his Master's kindest Thoughts to move.
We ne'er Lampoon'd his Conduct when employ'd
King *James's* Secret Counsels to divide:
Then we caress'd him as the only Man,
Which could the doubtful Oracle explain:
The only *Hushai* able to repel
The dark Designs of our *Achitophel*.
Compar'd his Master's Courage, to his Sense;
The Ablest Statesman, and the Bravest Prince.
Ten Years in *English* Service he appear'd,
And gain'd his Master's, and the World's Regard:
But 'Tis not England'*s Custom to Reward.*
The Wars are over, *England* needs him not;
Now he's a *Dutchman*, and *the Lord knows what.*   *Schonberg*, the Ablest
Soldier of his Age,
    With *Great Nassau* did in our Cause engage:
Both joyn'd for *England's* Rescue and Defence,
The greatest Captain, and the greatest Prince.
With what Applause his Stories did we tell?
Stories which *Europe's* Volumes largely swell.
We counted him an Army in our Aid:
Where he commanded, no Man was afraid.
His Actions with a constant Conquest shine,
From *Villa–Vitiosa* to the *Rhine.*
France, Flanders, Germany, his Fame confess;
And all the World was fond of him, but Us.
Our Turn first serv'd, we grudg'd him the Command.
Witness the Grateful Temper of the Land!   We blame the K— that he relies
too much
    On Strangers, *Germans, Hugonots*, and *Dutch*;
And seldom would his great Affairs of State,
To *English* Counsellors Communicate.
The Fact might very well be answer'd thus;
He has so often been betray'd by us,
He must have been a Madman to rely

34

THE True-Born Englishman: A SATYR

On *English* Gentlemen's Fidelity.
For laying other Arguments aside,
This Thought might mortifie our *English* Pride,
That Foreigners have faithfully Obey'd him,
And none but *Englishmen* have e'er Betray'd him.
They have our Ships and Merchants bought and sold,
And barter'd *English* Blood for Foreign Gold.
First to the *French* they sold our *Turky* –Fleet,
And Injur'd *Talmarsh* next, at *Camaret*.
The King himself is shelter'd from their Snares,
Not by his Merit, but the Crown he wears.
Experience tells us 'Tis the *English* way,
Their Benefactors always to betray.
　　And left Examples should be too remote,
A Modern Magistrate of Famous Note,
Shall give you his own History by Rote.
I'll make it out, deny it he that can,
His Worship is a *True–Born–Englishman*,
In all the Latitude that empty Word
By Modern Acceptation's understood.
The Parish–Books his Great Descent Record,
And now he hopes ere long to be a Lord.
And truly as things go, it would be pity
But such as he *should Represent* the City:
While Robb'ry for Burnt–Offering he brings,
And gives to God what he has stole from Kings:
Great Monuments of Charity he raises,
And good St. Magnus *whistles out his Praises.*
To City–Goals he grants a Jubilee,
And hires Huzza's from his own Mobilee.
　　Lately he wore the Golden Chain and Gown,
With which Equipp'd, he thus harangu'd the Town.

His Fine Speech, &c.

  With Clouted Iron Shoes, and Sheep–Skin Breeches,
More Rags than Manners, and more Dirt than Riches
From driving Cows and Calves to *Layton*–Market,
While of my Greatness there appear'd no Spark yet,
Behold I come, to let you see the Pride
With which Exalted Beggars always Ride.
  Born to the Needful Labours of the Plow,
The Cart–Whip Grac'd me, as the Chain does now.
Nature and Fate in doubt what Course to take,
Whether I shou'd a Lord or Plough–Boy make;
Kindly at last resolv'd they wou'd promote me,
And first *a Knave*, and then *a Knight* they Vote me.
What Fate appointed, Nature did prepare,
And furnish'd me with an exceeding Care.
To fit me for what they design'd to have me;
And ev'ry Gift *but Honesty* they gave me.
  And thus Equipp'd, to this Proud Town I came,
In quest of Bread, and not in quest of Fame.
Blind to my future Fate, a humble Boy,
Free from the *Guilt and Glory* I enjoy.
The Hopes which my Ambition entertain'd,
Were in the Name of *Foot–Boy*, all contain'd.
The Greatest Heights from Small Beginnings rise;
The Gods were Great on Earth, before they reach'd she Skies.
  B—well, the Generous Temper of whose Mind;
Was always to be bountiful inclin'd:
Whether by his ill Fate or Fancy led,
First took me up, and furnish'd me with Bread.
The little Services he put me to,
Seem'd Labours, rather than were truly so.
But always my Advancement he design'd;
For 'twas his very Nature to be kind.
Large was his Soul, his Temper ever free;
The best of Masters and of Men to me.
And I who was before decreed by Fate,

THE True–Born Englishman: A SATYR

To be made Infamous as well as Great,
With an obsequious Diligence obey'd him,
Till trusted with his All, and then betray'd him,   All his past
Kindnesses I trampled on,
Ruin'd his Fortunes to erect my own.
So Vipers in the Bosom bred, begin
To hiss at that Hand first which took them in.
With eager Treach'ry I his Fall pursu'd,
And my first Trophies were *Ingratitude*.

   Ingratitude, the worst of Humane Guilt;
The bafest Actior Mankind can commit;
Which like the Sin against the Holy Ghost,
Has least of Honour, and of Guilt the most;
Distinguish'd from all other Crimes by this,
That 'Tis a Crime which no Man will confess.
That Sin alone, which shou'd not be forgiv'n
On Earth, altho' perhaps it may in Heav'n.

sp;   Thus my first Benefactor I o'erthrew;
And how shou'd I be to a second true?
The Publick Trust came next into my Care,
And I to use them scurvily prepare:
My Needy Sov'reign Lord I play'd upon,
And lent him many a Thousand of his own;
For which great Int'rests I took care to Charge,
And so my ill–got Wealth became so large.

   My Predecessor *Judas* was a Fool,
Fitter to ha'been whipt and sent to School,
Than Sell a Saviour: Had I been at Hand,
His Master had not been so cheap trapann'd;
I would ha' made the eager *Jews* ha'found,
For Thirty Pieces, Thirty thousand Pound.

   My Cousin *Ziba*, of Immortal Fame,
(Ziba *and I shall never want a Name*:)
First–born of Treason, Nobly did advance
His Master's Fall, for his Inheritance.
By whose keen Arts old *David* first began

37

To break his sacred Oath to *Jonathan*:
The Good Old King 'Tis thought was very loth
To break his Word, and therefore broke his Oath.
Ziba's a Traytor of some Quality,
Yet *Ziba* might ha' been inform'd by me:
Had I been there, he ne'er had been Content
With half th' Estate, nor half the Government.
  In our late Revolution 'twas thought strange,
That I of all Mankind shou'd like the Change,
But they who wonder'd at it, never knew,
That in it I did my old Game pursue:
Nor had they heard of Twenty thousand Pound.
Which never yet was lost, nor ne'er was found.
  Thus all things in their turn to Sale I bring,
God and my Master first, and then the King:
Till by successful Villanies made Bold,
I thought to turn the Nation into Gold;
And so to Forg—y my Hand I bent,
Not doubting I cou'd gull the Government;
But there was ruffl'd by the Parliament.
And if I scap'd the unhappy Tree to Climb,
'Twas want of Law, and not for want of Crime.
  But my *Old Friend*, who Printed in my Face
A needful Competence of *English* Brass,
Having more Business yet for me to do,
And loth to lose his trusty Servant so,
Manag'd the Matter with such Art and Skill,
As sav'd his Hero, and threw out the B—ll.
  And now I'm Grac'd with unexpected Honours,
For which I'll certainly abuse the Donors:
Knighted. and made a Tribune of the People.
Whose Laws and Properties I'm like to keep well.
The *Custos Rotulorum* of the City,
And Captain of the Guards of their *Banditti*.
Surrounded by my Catchpoles, I'declare
Against the Needy Debtor open War.

I Hang poor Thieves for stealing of your Pelf,
And suffer none to Rob you, but my self.
sp;   The King Commanded me to help Reform ye,
And how I'll do't, Miss shall inform ye.
I keep the best Seraglio in the Nation,
And hope in time to bring it into Fashion.
No *Brimstone Whore* need fear the Lath from me.
That part I'll leave to Brother *Jeffery*.
Our Gallants need not go abroad to *Rome*,
I'll keep a Whoreing Jubilce at Home.
Whoring's the Darling of my Inclination;
A'n't I a Magistrate for Reformation?
For this my Praise is sung by ev'ry Bard,
For which *Bridewel* wou'd be a just Reward.
In Print my Panegyricks fill the Street,
And hired Goal–Birds their Huzza's Repeat.
Some Charities contriv'd to make a show,
Have taught the Needy Rabble to do so;
Whose empty Noise is a Mechanick Fame,
Since for Sir *Belzebub* they'd do the same.

The Conclusion.

Then let us boast of Ancestors no more,
Or Deeds of Heroes done in Days of Yore,
In latent Records of the Ages past,
Behind the Rear of Time, in long Oblivion plac'd.
For if our Virtues must in Lines descend,
The Merit with the Families would end:
And Intermixtures would most fatal grow;
For Vice would be Hereditary too;
The tainted Blood wou'd of Necessity,
In voluntary Wickedness convey.
Vice, like Ill–Nature, for an Age or two,
May seem a Generation to pursue:

But Virtue seldom does regard the Breed;
Fools do the Wise, and Wise Men Fools succeed.
What is't to us, what Ancestors we had?
If Good, what better? Or what worse, if Bad?
Examples are for Imitation set,
Yet all Men follow Virtue with Regret.
  Cou'd but our Ancestors retrieve their Fate,
And see their Off-spring thus Degenerate;
How we contend for Birth and Names unknown,
And Build on their past Actions, not our own;
They'd Cancel Records, and their Tombs Deface,
And openly disown the Vile Degenerate Race:
For Fame of Families is all a Cheat,
'Tis Personal Virtue only makes us Great.

Printed in the United Kingdom
by Lightning Source UK Ltd.
121654UK00001B/97/A